First published in Great Britain in 1993
by Simon & Schuster Young Books
Campus 400
Maylands Avenue
Hemel Hempstead
Herts HP2 7EZ

Text © 1993 Pat Moon
Illustrations © 1993 Peter Kavanagh

Typeset in 15/23pt Souvenir Light by Goodfellow & Egan Ltd, Cambridge
Printed and bound in Portugal by Ediçoes ASA

British Library Cataloguing in Publication Data available

ISBN 0 7500 1355 9
ISBN 0 7500 1356 7 (pbk)

PAT MOON

the Trouble with Mice

Illustrated by Peter Kavanagh

SIMON & SCHUSTER
YOUNG BOOKS

It all began the day that Grandad came home with the cage. He found it on the pavement where it had been put out with the rubbish bags for the dustmen. Now it sits in the corner of the kitchen.

Mary sits at the table, where Mum and Nan are having a cup of tea. She struggles with sticky, sore fingers to push a needle through the stiff material of her needlework picture.

It has to be finished for the class display on Open Day next week. It is meant to be a butterfly but her brother Chris says it looks more like a pterodactyl.

The more Mary works on her picture the more she thinks Chris is right.

Mary looks at the cage. Its rusty bars are dented at the top, as if a giant has trodden on it. A square hole gapes where the door should be.

"Looks to me about as useful as a chocolate teapot," says Nan, peering over her teacup.

Mary pricks her finger for the third time. She would like to cut the cloth into a hundred pieces.

She hears the back gate crash against its latch. Chris is home from school. He ambles in and throws down his bag, helps himself to a mug of tea and tips back on his chair.

Mary waits for him to spot the cage.

"What's that?" he asks at last.

"Your grandad found it," says Mum.

"Cor, great," says Chris examining it.

"Now I can get my mouse."

"Oh no, you can't. I'm not having vermin in this house."

"But Mum . . ."

"And that's final."

"Go on, Mum. It's only a mouse. White mice aren't vermin. You ought to see Ben's. They don't smell, honest."

All week he talks about mice.

He straightens the bars on the cage and scrubs it out. And Grandad makes a little door and fixes it on with wire.

"Please, Mum. I'll keep it in the shed. You won't even see it. Mice are nice when you get to know them . . ."

"I'll give you mice if you don't shut up!" Mum threatens.

"Great!" he yells. "Then I'll go on, and on, and on, and on . . ." He ducks the tea-towel that she throws at him.

Mary knows he'll get his way: somehow he always does.

11

Then on Friday
at teatime, Chris
remembers
the letter
from school.

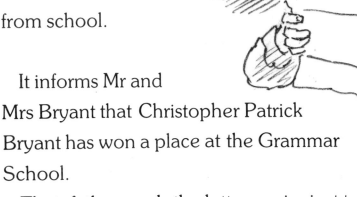

It informs Mr and
Mrs Bryant that Christopher Patrick
Bryant has won a place at the Grammar
School.

Their father reads the letter again, just to be
certain.

"Well done, Chris," says Dad.

"Ben's passed too," says Chris.

He pauses before adding, "They're giving him a new mountain bike."

He waits and watches.

His parents swap glances.

"A bike, eh," says Dad. "I don't think we could manage a new bike."

"There is something else," says Chris. "I wouldn't mind a mouse. Ben says I can have one of his litter for one pound fifty, and there'll be a few other things I'll need, like a feeding bottle and bedding and . . ."

"Well, that's settled then," says Dad.

Mum glares at him and her mouth gathers like a drawstring bag. She starts to clear the table.

"Filthy things," she says. "Just you make sure it stays in that shed. I don't want its business in my house."

Grandad gives Chris a wink.

CHAPTER TWO

Mickey Mouse moved in a week later. Chris has painted his name on to a strip of wood and he's fixing it to the front of the cage. A tiny pink nose is twitching at it through the bars.

"See," says Chris. "He knows his name already. Good boy. Mickey, Mickey."

He offers Mickey a seed.
"I'm training him, see.
If I repeat his name
every time I feed him,
he'll soon get the idea.
Mickey, Mickey."

He trains him to sit on his head, run up his sleeve
and inside his shirt, sit in his pocket and walk along
a length of string.

"Mum'll kill you," says Mary when he takes him out from his pocket and sets him on the table.
They watch him wrinkling his nose at a breadcrumb and standing up on tiny feet, resting tiny pink paws against the jam jar.

Chris scoops him up and sits innocently with his hand beneath the table as Mum returns with the teapot.

"I think I might get another mouse," he announces.

"Then you've got another think coming," says Mum.

"Ben's is having another litter. She had nine last time and he made nearly seven pounds. I think I might go into business."

"Not in this house, you won't," says Mum.

18

"Please, Anna," begs Mary. "I'll show you Mickey Mouse if I can have one."

"All right, then."

Anna hands over a sherbet lemon and they wander out to the shed.

"I'm looking after him while Chris is at scout camp," says Mary.

She picks up a seed and calls, "Mickey, Mickey."

His whiskery snout pokes out from the dense bed of shavings he has made in the jam jar in the corner. He tests the air and trots over to take his reward.

"Can I hold him?" asks Anna.

"I shouldn't let him out really."

"You're scared."

"Am not."

"You can have another sherbet lemon."

Mary turns the little handle on the cage door and scoops Mickey into her palm. He peers over the edge of her hand into the abyss below.

"You can stroke him if you like," says Mary.

"But I want to hold him."

"You might drop him."

"I won't."

"Promise? God's honour?"

Mary watches anxiously as Anna lets him walk up her sweatshirt and on to her shoulder.

"I've got to put him back now," pleads Mary.

"Spoilsport."

Mary returns Mickey to his prison, and sighs with relief.

CHAPTER THREE

It can't be, thinks Mary. She stares in disbelief. For a second she cannot move. She closes her eyes and opens them again, hoping she is wrong. But she's not. The door of Mickey's cage is open. I shut it properly, I'm sure I shut it properly, she thinks. But she can't remember exactly.

She slams the shed door shut and rushes over to the cage.

"Mickey! Mickey!"

Any minute now his twitching pink nose will appear. Any minute now. "Mickey! Mickey!"

22

She peers into the cage, reaches her hand through the door, turning over the shavings. Then she lifts out the jam jar and tips it out, pulling with her fingers at the bedding. There are seeds and shreds of lettuce and droppings: but no Mickey.

The worst has happened. She has let Mickey escape. No, she thinks, the worst *hasn't* happened. The worst will happen on Friday when Chris gets back.

She stands, shoulders hunched, hands clasped to her mouth. Please God, let me find him. Please!

"You were a long time," says Mum.
"I was cleaning up the cage a bit."
"Then you wash those hands this minute."

Mary keeps returning to the shed where she thinks she sees a little ear poking out over a flower pot, or a little tail from behind a watering can. But it is only a scrap of paper, or a piece of wire.

She starts to see mice everywhere. She worries about treading on Mickey, and she walks with her head down, staring at the ground.

"What's the matter with you?" asks Mum. "You've a face like a week of wet Sundays. Have you been quarrelling with Anna again?"

It is when she is coming back from the corner shop with the loaf of bread Mum sent her for, that she decides what to do. She runs towards the pet shop. She can't take too long or Mum will start to worry.

She doesn't see the tropical fish and the
parrot that usually set her dreaming. She only
sees the cage of white mice. The label says
"WHITE MICE
£2.50 EACH".

Two pounds fifty?
Where is she going
to get two pounds
fifty before Friday?

WHITE
MICE
£2-50
each

"Mary, this change is 20p short," says Mum as they sit down to dinner.

"I must have dropped it," lies Mary.

She keeps her head down to hide the blush of guilt.

Is keeping change as bad as stealing? Even when it's for a good reason? It feels the same.

"Oh, Mary, you must try to be more careful," says Mum.
It makes her feel even worse.

"Do you need any errands?" Mary asks
Grandad.

"I'll want the afternoon paper, and I'm
running short of peppermints," he answers.

"But it'll wait."

"I don't mind," says Mary. "I can go now – I
might be busy later."

Mum looks at her suspiciously.

"Run upstairs then," he says, "and fetch a
pound from my room."

There are pound coins, fifty pence pieces, tens, twenties and fives, all arranged in neat piles on the mantelpiece. They turn into rows of white mice with curly pink tails. She picks up a pound and runs downstairs. Grandad always gives her something when she runs errands.

"You spoil her," says her mother when Mary returns with the paper and sweets and he gives her a 20p.

In her bedroom,
Mary lifts the lid off the
china rabbit where she keeps
her money and   tips it out
on to the bed.

She counts it carefully
and then again, just to be sure.
With Grandad's 20p
and Mum's change of 20p
it makes £1.50 altogether.

She still has to find a pound.

"Mary! I'm popping over to see your nan,"
calls Mum from the foot of the stairs. "Can you
set the table for tea before I get back?"

As soon as she hears the gate click, Mary rushes down. Grandad is in the garden bending over the lettuces. She pulls the cushions off the settee and plunges her hands down the sides and back. She finds a safety pin, a pencil, a hair slide, half a biscuit and a whole 20p.

That leaves just eighty pence to find. Surely she can find the rest, just eighty pence?

She tries all
her pockets,
her old purse,
her rucksack
and the pots on
the kitchen dresser
where she finds
a 10p in the teapot
that looks like a cottage.

Seventy pence now and she'll be all right.
It's not such a lot. But at this moment it may
as well be seventy pounds.

She sits on her bed,
chin on hands, trawling her
mind for places to look.

Then she remembers
Chris's money box.

She reaches to the top of his cupboard for the china pig with the cork stopper then tips it on to the bed. She cannot believe it: a five pound note, six pound coins, and handfuls of 50ps and other coins. She counts out seventy pence and quickly scoops the rest back. She will pay it back. As soon as she can, she will pay it back.

CHAPTER FOUR

"Mickey! Mickey!" calls Mary as she holds a sunflower seed against the bars. But the new mouse has buried itself inside the jam jar.

Mary has not thought of this. She remembered to ask for a male mouse, and picked the one that she thought looked most like Mickey. But she had forgotten about Mickey's acrobatics and friendliness. This Mickey squeaks and squeals and shakes and tries to nip her finger.

She carries him around in the garden, anxiously
stroking him and repeating his name. She puts
him on her sleeve, but he just clings, quivering.

She must have an answer ready. "He's out of
practice," she will say. "I didn't take him out
too much, just in case. You'll have to re-train
him."

When Chris walks in
from scout camp
on Friday evening,
he looks as if
he hasn't washed
for a week.
Mum sends him
straight upstairs
to have a bath.

Mary waits nervously
as she hears the water
running into the bath.
All too soon, he's out,
clean and changed
and running down
the stairs. Then he's out
through the back door
and into the shed.

"Mickey, Mickey," she hears him call.

Surely they can hear her heart pounding? It feels as if any moment it will burst out of her shirt, popping the buttons in all directions.

Then, just seconds later, she can see Chris through the window, leaning against the sill, stroking Mickey. Then the mouse is running up his arm on to his head, and Chris has tied the string to the drain pipe and the mouse is balancing along as if he's been doing it all his life . . .

It is true, thinks Mary.
Miracles do still happen.
And the pounding
in her chest lessens
just a little. She
moves away from
the window.

But not very far, because there is a shout
from the shed and Chris is running out – and
he has two mice, one in each hand.

"I don't believe it," he's shouting. "Look,
Mum. There's two of them!"

Mum stops from hanging the groundsheet over the washing line to dry. She is studying Mary's staring face at the window. And Mary is trying to work out how and when Mickey The First might have found his way back to the cage.

"Mary! Come here this minute!" shouts her mother.

Slowly, Mary edges out.

"What do you know about this?" Mum asks.

Mary stares down at her trainers.

"Come on, Mary," says Mum. "I want an answer."

"I thought he looked lonely, that's all," cries Mary her mind spinning. "I thought he'd like a friend. So I saved up and bought him."

Mum gives Mary a long look.

"Are you telling me the truth, Mary?"

Mary chews her lip.

"You should have asked me first, Mary," says Mum. "If you really wanted a mouse so much, you should have said so, not gone behind my back like this. I knew something was up."

Mary narrows her eyes
at Chris who is silently
watching from the path,
holding the mice.
She won't cry.
She won't give in.
Not yet.

"I'm very disappointed
in you, Mary,"
says Mum as she pegs
the groundsheet in place.

But Mary is running, up the stairs and into her bedroom where she sobs till she has no tears left.

That was five weeks ago. Two weeks ago,
Mickey The First had a litter of eight, tiny,
naked mice.

"She must have been a Minnie all the time,"
says Chris as he alters her name tag.

Mary decided she doesn't really like mice so
she let Chris buy Mickey The Second from her
for one pound fifty, but only after he'd agreed
to sharing the money he got from selling the
mouse babies.

He's renamed Mickey the Second. There's a new name tag on the cage now. It says DENNIS THE MENACE.

The pet shop bought the mouse babies for 70p each, so even after Mary had sneaked back the 70p to Chris's money box and 20p to Mum's purse, she still had three pounds forty to put into her china rabbit.

Chris says he wants
hamsters next but Mum
says she is definitely
putting her foot down
about hamsters.

STORYBOOKS

Look out for other books in the Storybooks series:

Sam and Sue and Lavatory Lou
Robert Swindells
Illustrated by Val Biro

When Sam and Sue go to the funfair, the biggest fright they get is when Sam goes to the Gents, and finds a ghost!

Mandy's Mermaid
Anne Forsyth
Illustrated by Thelma Lambert

Mandy has always dreamt of meeting a mermaid, but when she discovers one on the beach, the mermaid isn't quite what she had expected.

The Birthday Phone
Toby Forward
Illustrated by Neil Reed

Helen isn't very happy with her birthday presents, so she decides to call the Birthday Fairy and complain. Nobody believes Helen when she says she's spoken to the Birthday Fairy, but Helen knows she really exists.

Dreamy Daniel, Brainy Bert
Scoular Anderson

Daniel is always getting into trouble at school for daydreaming. But together with the class mouse, Brainy Bert, Daniel overcomes his problem.

Hopping Mad
Nick Warburton
Illustrated by Tony Blundell

Janey's little brother, Martin, is clumsy, stupid and useless. But he has one special talent: he is very good at jumping around in a duvet cover. Quick-thinking Janey soon finds a use for Martin's ability.

If you would like to order any of these books, or find out more about Simon & Schuster Young Books's Storybooks series, write to: The Sales Department, Simon & Schuster Young Books, Campus 400, Maylands Avenue, Hemel Hempstead HP2 7EZ.